Benjamin Bear
Says Please

CANDLE
BOOKS

Other titles in this series:
BENJAMIN BEAR SAYS SORRY
BENJAMIN BEAR SAYS THANK YOU

BENJAMIN BEAR SAYS PLEASE
Copyright © 2007 Lion Hudson plc/
Tim Dowley Associates

Designed by Jen Warren

Published in 2007 by Candle Books
(a publishing imprint of Lion Hudson plc).

Distributed in the UK by Marston Book Services Ltd,
PO Box 269, Abingdon, Oxon OX14 4YN
Distributed in the USA by Kregel Publications,
Grand Rapids, Michigan 49501

Worldwide co-edition produced by Lion Hudson plc,
Wilkinson House, Jordan Hill Road,
Oxford OX2 8DR England
Tel:+44 (0) 1865 302750   Fax: +44 (0) 1865 302757
email:coed@lionhudson.com   www.lionhudson.com

ISBN 978-1-85985-678-9 (UK)
ISBN 978-0-8254-7343-2 (USA)

Printed in China

Benjamin Bear
Says Please

Claire Freedman
Illustrated by Steve Smallman

One morning Benjamin Bear woke up feeling extra bouncy!

"Hooray, it's been snowing!" he shouted excitedly. "Everything's covered in white."

Benjamin tugged on his bright red boots and rushed outside to play.

Down by the frosty pine trees, Benjamin saw his friends, Fizzy and Stripe.

They were building the biggest snowman Benjamin had ever seen.

"Wow, that looks fun!" Benjamin said. "I love building snowmen."

Before Stripe and Fizzy had time to say anything, Benjamin began scooping up piles of sparkling snow for their snowman's head.

"We're happy for you to help us," Fizzy told Benjamin, as the little bear added some twigs for the snowman's arms. "But it is polite to say please first."

Ooops! *"Fizzy and Stripe are right,"* Benjamin thought to himself. *"I must remember to say please next time."*

After building their snowman,
Benjamin and his friends scrunched
through the deep snow and up the hill.

Wheee! Suddenly Flop-Ear whizzed
past them on her brand new sledge.

"That looks great fun, Flop-Ear!" Benjamin cried bouncily. "I bet I could make your sledge go even faster!"

Before Flop-Ear could say a word, Benjamin had jumped aboard the sledge.

He held onto Flop-Ear tightly as they raced downhill together.

"Of course you can ride on my sledge with me, Benjamin," Flop-Ear said breathlessly as they reached the bottom. "But it is polite to say please first."

"*Oh no, I forgot again,*" Benjamin thought to himself. "*I really must remember to say please next time.*"

As Benjamin Bear was bouncing through the thick snowdrifts, he spotted his friend Hoppy.

Hoppy had found a big patch of ice under the trees, and was happily slipping and sliding on it.

"What a great skating rink." Benjamin called out. "It looks lovely and slippery. I'd like a go!"

Benjamin rushed across and slithered straight onto
the ice. Very soon he fell over in a laughing heap.
Hoppy helped him up.

"You're welcome to slide on my ice patch with me," Hoppy told Benjamin. "But it is polite to say please first."

"*Oh,*" Benjamin thought to himself. "*I really meant to say please this time. How ever could I have forgotten again?*"

After a great time building snowmen, sledging downhill and sliding on the ice, Benjamin and his friends were feeling very hungry.

"Look!" Benjamin cried. "Snippy has set up a food stall down by the frozen stream."

Everyone's eyes lit up.

Snippy was soon handing round hot sugared doughnuts and steaming mugs of hot chocolate to everyone.

The little bear couldn't wait!

He scrunched across the snow as fast as his red boots could take him.

"Yummy, I'd love a delicious doughnut," he told Snippy. Benjamin held out his paw to take one, when suddenly… "Oh, I've just remembered something very important," he smiled.

"Please can I have a doughnut and a hot chocolate, Snippy?" Benjamin asked.

Snippy smiled. "Of course you can Benjamin – especially after you said please so nicely."

"Hooray!" cheered Benjamin happily, taking a big bite.
Soon everyone was tucking in and enjoying themselves.

"Benjamin," said his friends, as snowflakes began to fall. "Will you come out and play in the snow with us tomorrow? PLEASE – it's been such fun."

"Of course!" Benjamin laughed, thinking he'd like nothing better. "Seeing that you asked me so politely."

And although it was cold and snowy outside, inside Benjamin Bear felt happy and warm. And full of bounce!

When there's something that you'd like,
It's good to be polite.
If you always say "please" first,
You know you've got it right!